D1367202

DATE
TODAY

INTERGALACTIC IDOL

Samit Basu
Malavika P. C.

I know I am in trouble and I know you might not believe what I am about to tell you. But I swear that all of this is true.

I could have got out of trouble by inventing some convenient and completely believable lie, but you know I'm not like that.

Okay, maybe you don't know I'm not like that, but it's true.

You probably don't believe in aliens but if you'd just listen to me, you'd realize that after what I've been through, your disbelief means nothing to me.

I could have died. I could have been stranded on a galaxy a gazillion light years away from here. Worst of all, I could have been married.

Anyway, this is my story.

One Thursday evening, I was sitting quietly at my desk, doing my **math homework.** Really!
That's what I was doing – Second-Order Differential Equations, problems 12 to 47!

Suddenly, I heard a loud roaring noise followed by a huge **crash.**

I raced out to the balcony and downstairs to the lawn, carrying my math notebook with my homework in it.

I paused only to gulp and catch my breath because what I saw was something that I had never ever seen before.

In the garden, right in front of me was a huge smoking crater with a bright yellow **spaceship** in the middle.

The thing that came out of the spaceship did not look like any alien that I had ever seen on television. It looked like a pelican, except that it had two beaks, tentacles instead of wings and spirally things like springs for feet. It bounced out of the ship and landed in front of me.

What could I do? I saluted it. 'Welcome to our planet,' I said. 'I mean you no harm.'

'My name is Ynos Bandmanager V2.6,' it said, 'and I need your help.'

Boing BOING BOING BOING BOING BOING BOING BOING

Ynos told me many things. I'll summarize briefly – I had to go with it to the planet Arkstaro Two, where Intergalactic Idol, this **intergalactic music contest** was happening. And I had to be our galaxy's champion.

If I won, I would have everything I ever wanted and be an intergalactic **celebrity**.

If I didn't go, our galaxy, which obviously included Earth, would be in violation of an intergalactic peace treaty, and would be destroyed.

'Why me?' I asked.

'It wasn't supposed to be you,' said Ynos. 'But my ship crashed, as you can see, and once I repair it, I won't have enough fuel or enough time to find the best singer on your planet. So it has to be you.'

Ynos gave me a look full of disgust and despair or maybe joy. It's hard to tell with a double-beaked tentacled pelican on springs.

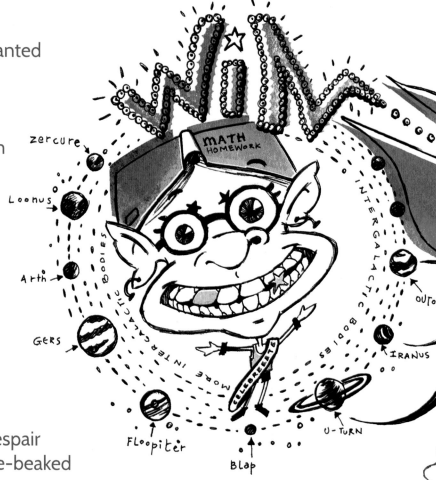

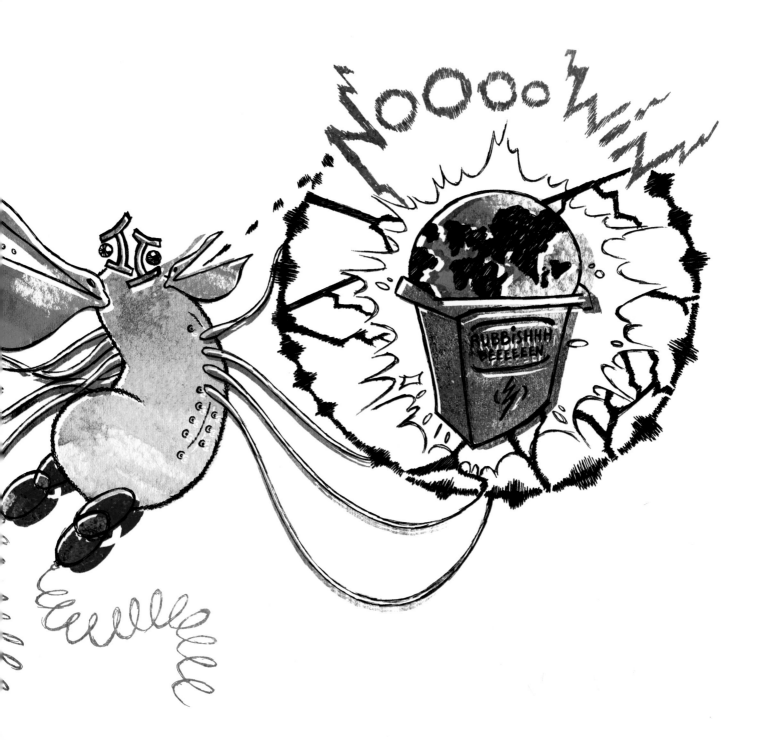

Ynos' ship suddenly emitted a loud beep, rose and started hovering mid-air. Ynos uttered some sort of strange command, and the ship started clicking and humming.

'But why our planet in the first place?' I asked. 'Aren't there better singers anywhere else in our galaxy?'

'I have no time for this stupid discussion,' said Ynos. 'Come with me.'

Still clutching my math notebook, I got into the ship, which Ynos had miraculously repaired with some strange commands.

EARTH

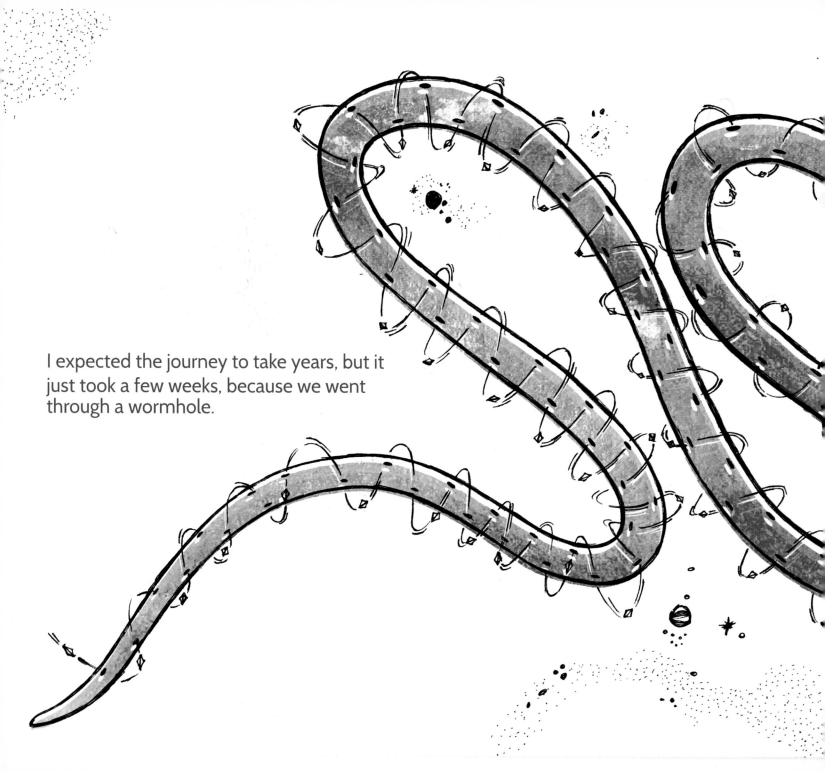

I expected the journey to take years, but it just took a few weeks, because we went through a wormhole.

On the way, Ynos explained the intricacies of wormhole travel technology to me, but I have forgotten them because my humble school student's mind is not equipped to deal with such complicated matters.

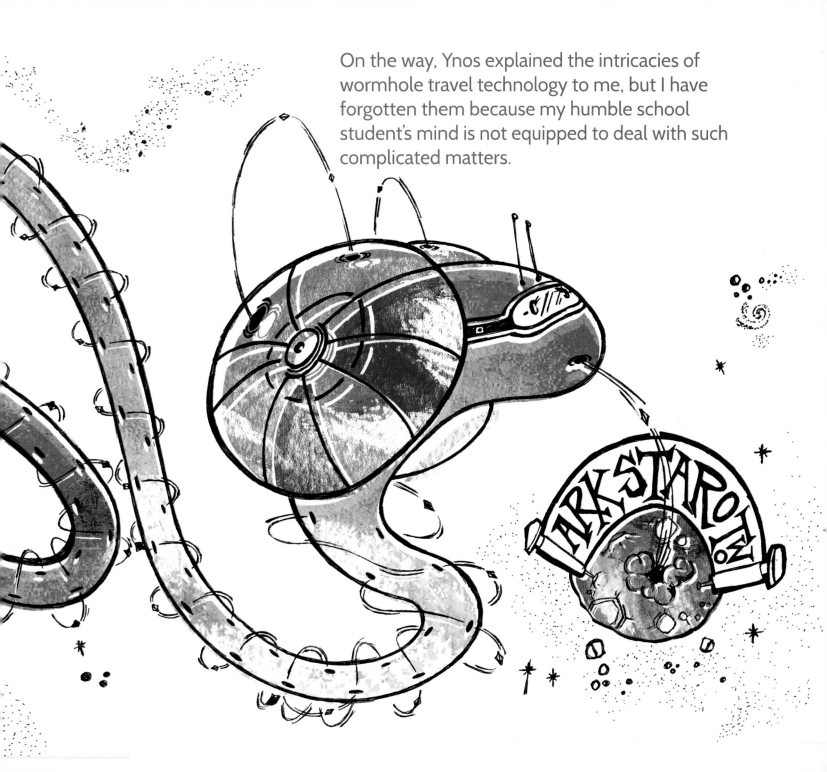

We had so many adventures on our way. We almost got sucked into a planet-leech and we got into a space dogfight with Pudavulerian terrorists.

One day, I'd like to tell you about all these adventures.

We reached Arkstaro Two just in time for the contest, but in the middle of having space adventures, I'd completely forgotten one rather important fact, which hit me like several comets on the morning of the contest.

The fact was this: I can't sing. At all. It's not one of my skills. Sorry.

The contest was held in this magnificent amphitheatre, so large that from the huge stage I couldn't even see the far end. People and things from hundreds of planets had come to see this.

What do I tell you about the creatures I saw?

I saw elephant-like beings with butterfly wings, giant snakes of pure light called tutus and aerosol sprays containing beings that were pure smell.

I saw humanoids of every possible colour, some with multiple heads, others with animal or metallic parts.

I saw robots, talking umbrellas and a huge variety of metallic, plastic, liquid, gaseous and even pure energy beings.

There were five contestants and three judges. Each had one song to sing. I was supposed to sing third.

The first contestant was a **sound-assassin** from Homisonic. You know that sound travels in waves, right? Like vibrations through the air? Well, the sound-assassins of Homisonic know how to use these sound waves to transfer lethal physical force.

And so, within seconds of the first song, two of my fellow contestants were headless.

Luckily, I was bending down to tie my shoelaces at the time, and the fifth contestant wasn't listening, because she was busy signing autographs. And before the sound-assassin could really focus on us, security troopers gagged her and dragged her away.

aaaiiieee

THE
SOUND
ASSASSIN

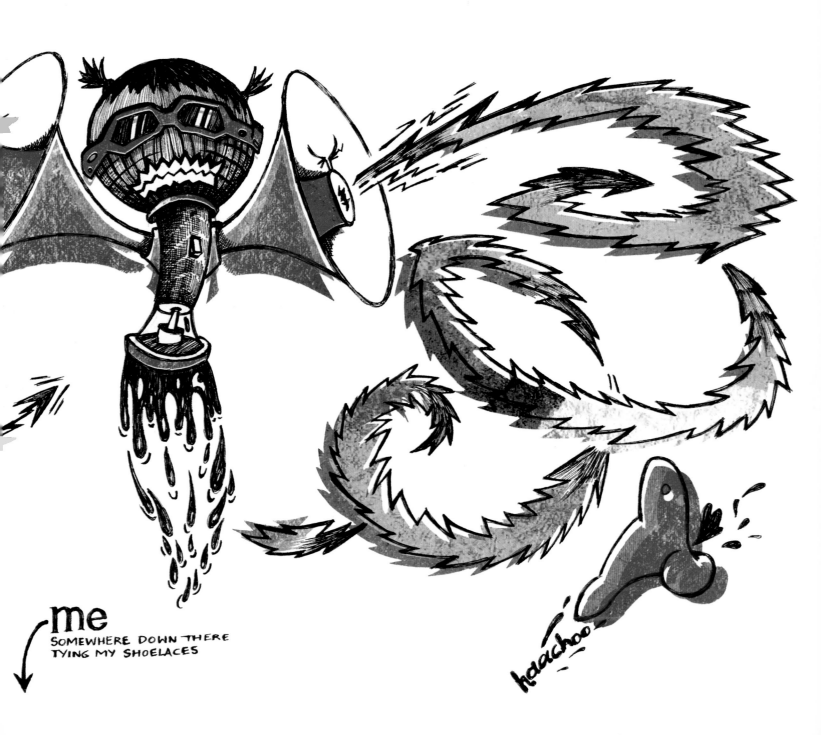

me
SOMEWHERE DOWN THERE
TYING MY SHOELACES

haachoo

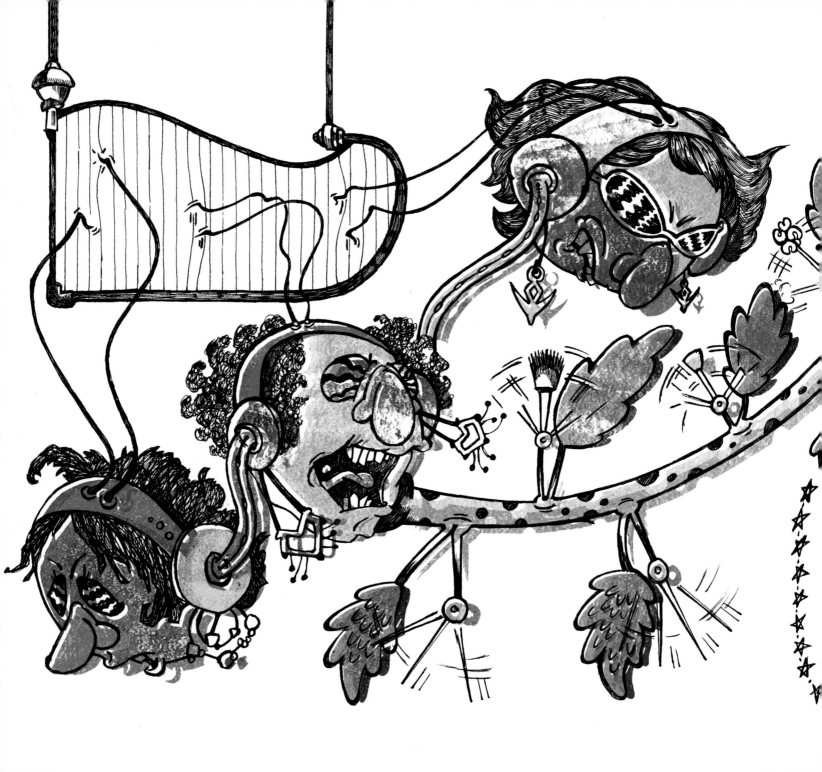

Now suddenly there were just two contestants left, and my chances of winning the whole contest were dramatically increased.

I was next. I sang a **Bollywood** song and I have to confess I did a terrible job.

My opponent had unfair advantages. She had three heads, all singing different tunes (and singing them strangely well), not to mention arms like drumsticks which beat lovely rhythms on the thin skin of her wings, and antennae that played one another like a harp.

She was, I learned later, the intergalactic champion, three contests running, and her name was The Supreme Space Opera Diva, Motlimixa III. And she was only about two million times better than me by any standards.

She won. I came second.

It was rigged, I tell you. These contests always are.

But there was a **bigger** problem.

It turned out that the daughter of Oogba Lopp of Stimblepok, the most powerful **mafia don** in the eastern part of our galaxy, was in **love** with me. Apparently my soulful singing had melted her heart, which must have been pretty melty in the first place, because she was basically this giant slug.

Also, I had, she claimed, looked in her direction throughout my performance which, according to ancient Stimblepok tradition, meant that we were married.

DAUGHTER (OF)— Oogba Lopp

marriage
by sight

How did I get out of this situation? Well, it involved a thimble, a lot of salt, a certain amount of grovelling, a lot of blackmail, and a very difficult two days hidden inside a crate full of poisonous lobsters.

I'll tell you exactly what happened another day.

a thimble

LOT OF
SALT

me

the infamous
crate of POiSONOUS
LOBSTERS

Finally, Ynos put me in his ship and told me that thanks to
the brilliance of wormhole-travel technology, I would be
restored to earth around the same time I left it,
so I wouldn't lose any time in school at all.

And then things suddenly went wrong again. There was
a little leak in the ship's fuel tank, which meant that we
were a few hours off schedule.

A comet left a tiny hole in the outer membrane of the ship,
and since I didn't want to be sucked out into the great
vacuum of space and spend eternity trying to hitchhike a
ride from passing spaceships, I stuffed the nearest
available object into the hole.

Unfortunately, this turned out to be my math notebook.

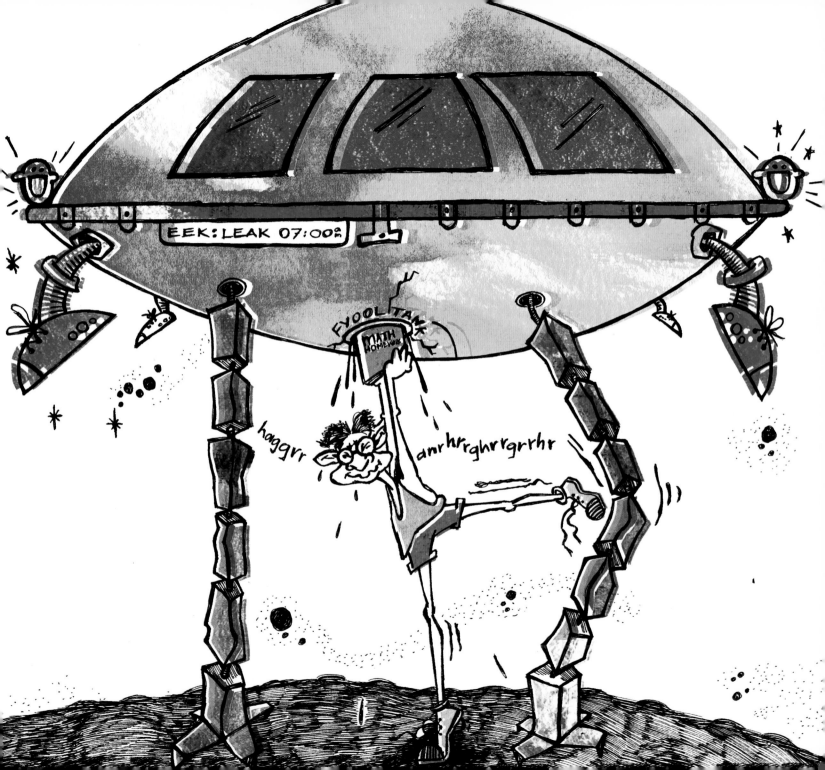

Ynos did drop me home, but this morning, not yesterday evening.

So, I just had time to brush my teeth, take a shower, change into my school uniform, comb my hair and come straight to school.

And that, Mrs. Gupta, is why I don't have my math homework with me today.

InterGalactic Idol

Text: Samit Basu
Illustrations: Malavika P. C.

Karadi Tales Company Pvt. Ltd.
3A Dev Regency 11 First Main Road Gandhinagar Adyar Chennai 600020
Ph: +91 44 4205 4243 Email: contact@karaditales.com
Website: www.karaditales.com

Distributed in North America by Consortium Book Sales & Distribution
The Keg House 34 Thirteenth Avenue NE Suite 101 Minneapolis MN 55413-1006 USA
Orders – Ph: (+1) 731-423-1550 Email: orderentry@perseusbooks.com
Electronic ordering via PUBNET (SAN 631760X) Website: www.cbsd.com

Printed in India
ISBN: 978-81-8190-257-3

Samit Basu is an award-winning writer, who has been published by Titan Books and Hachette India. His bestselling novels that form the Gameworld Trilogy marked the beginning of Indian English fantasy writing. Basu has also written for films and comics.

Malavika P. C. is an artist who works with multiple mediums – Illustration, Design, Performance, Play. Whichever be the medium, children invariably form the centre of her expression. Her illustrations for them are particularly filled with cheeky humour and general wickedness.

DATE
TODAY